CHAPTER ONE

"Come on, Honey!" cried Freya as Honey, her unicorn, weaved in and out of a row of upright poles. Bending round the final pole, Honey raced towards a table with two beanbags on it and a large hoop on the ground. Freya could hear her friends from Diamond dorm cheering them on.

"Go, Freya! Go, Honey!"

"You're in the lead! We can win!"

"Miss the hoop!" chanted the boys from Topaz dorm as Honey skidded to a halt by the table. Freya ignored them. Leaning down and grabbing the first beanbag, she aimed carefully and threw

it into the hoop on the ground. Honey nudged the next beanbag closer to Freya's hand with her nose and Freya threw that one into the hoop too. "Thanks!" she gasped as Honey set off, galloping determinedly towards a tall tube standing in the grass.

It was a Sunday afternoon and Diamond and Topaz dorms were holding an obstacle race in the grounds of Unicorn Academy. The two dorms got on really well and hung out a lot. They'd set the course up together. The fastest to finish would win but time was being added on for every mistake each unicorn-and-rider pair made. So far, Honey and Freya hadn't got anything wrong!

Reaching the tube, Freya threw herself from Honey's back. She'd been looking forward to this challenge! The tube had a small white ball inside it and the rider had to somehow get it out of the tube without touching it and put it into a cup.

There were two long-handled spoons beside it. Everyone else had taken ages to release the ball using only the spoons, as they kept dropping it. Freya loved making things work and this was her kind of challenge.

"I need water!" she told Honey as she dismounted. "Can you get some from the bird bath? As much as you can!"

Not stopping to ask why, Honey galloped to the bird bath, filled her mouth until her cheeks bulged and galloped back.

Freya pointed to the tube. "In there, Honey!"

Honey spat a stream of water into the tube. As the tube filled up, the ball was pushed upwards. When it reached the top, Freya scooped it out with one of the spoons and tossed it into the cup. It had taken almost no time at all.

"We did it!" she cried, jumping on to Honey's back.

The two of them raced across the finishing line

with Honey's long red and gold mane and tail streaming out behind her.

"Freya won by miles!" shouted Rosa, who had been timing Freya's round along with Miki from Topaz dorm. "Diamond dorm are the best!" she whooped.

Freya and Honey were quickly surrounded by the rest of Diamond dorm and their unicorns.

"That was brilliant!" exclaimed Matilda,

throwing her arms round Freya. Freya wriggled away. She didn't really like hugging or being hugged.

"You were so clever on that last challenge," said Ariana.

"I can't believe you thought to use water to get the ball out," Violet agreed.

Freya grinned. "It was fun, wasn't it, Honey?"

Honey whinnied in agreement.

"Rematch!" shouted Himmat from Topaz dorm. "Let's go again."

"OK," said Rosa eagerly. "You're on!"

"Count me out," said Freya. "It's been great, but I've got stuff to do."

"Your big secret invention?" asked Violet.

Freya nodded.

"Oh," Honey complained. "Can't we stay, Freya. Please? You can work on your invention another time."

"No, I really need to do some now," Freya said, dismounting and giving Honey a pat. "You can stay though." Honey didn't know yet that the secret project was a present for her birthday in just three days' time and Freya still had lots of work to do on it.

"It won't be the same without you," Honey said, nudging her with her nose. "Please stay?"

But Freya wouldn't be persuaded. She said goodbye and hurried back through the gardens towards the school. Her invention – a robotic unicorn that would bring Honey treats whenever she wanted – had been inspired by the automated trolleys that trundled around the stables moving hay bales. It had seemed the perfect way for Freya to combine her love of engineering with showing Honey how much she loved her. She couldn't wait to see her reaction when she saw it!

Maybe she'll be so pleased we'll even bond,

thought Freya hopefully. All the students at Unicorn Academy were paired with a unicorn when they first arrived, and they spent a year at the academy training to be guardians of wonderful Unicorn Island. During that year, the unicorn usually discovered their special magic power and bonded with their rider. Rosa, Ariana and Matilda in Diamond dorm had already found their unicorns' powers and bonded with them but Freya and Honey and Violet and Twinkle were still waiting.

Freya hurried towards the school, her mind focused on her invention. When she was near the end of a project, it was like having an itch she couldn't scratch until it was done. There were just a few problems to sort out now. The robot was working but it didn't look right yet and it still wasn't moving properly. *I need to stop it bumping into things and spinning to the left*, she thought.

But how?

The buildings of Unicorn Academy looked beautiful in the golden autumn sunlight. The marble and glass school glittered brightly but Freya barely noticed. Deep in thought, she headed for the little room next to the art studio that she had been using as her workshop. It was time to get to work again!

CHAPTER TWO

"Freya!" A banging on the workshop door made Freya jump and drop her spanner. She glanced at the clock on the wall. She'd been working on her robot for two hours. The time had flown by!

"FREYA!"

Recognising Rosa's voice, Freya ran to the door and opened it a crack. "What is it?" she asked.

"Can I come in?" Rosa demanded.

"No!" Freya held the door tightly. Seeing Rosa's

frown, she added, "Sorry, it's just I want to keep this invention secret because it's Honey's birthday present." She didn't want to risk anyone accidentally telling Honey about the robot before her birthday and ruining the surprise. Freya squeezed out through the door and shut it behind her. "What's going on?"

"Matilda's had a brilliant idea," Rosa said. "You know everyone at school's been a bit freaked out and tense ever since the camping trip?"

Freya nodded. The students had gone on a camping trip in Dingleberry Dell a couple of months ago. It had been really good fun until Diamond dorm had discovered that the ancient Heart Tree at the centre of the dell was being drained of its magic. A cloaked woman had appeared and attacked Matilda and her unicorn, Pearl. They had managed to scare her off, but who the figure was and why she had been draining the

Heart Tree remained a mystery. It wasn't the only strange incident either. A few months before that, Diamond dorm had discovered that someone had been draining a magic waterfall in the forest. The teachers still had no idea who the villain was, and all the students were on edge. What if they struck again?

"Well, Matilda thought that we should organise a big midnight party in the stables to help everyone relax and give them something else to think about," said Rosa. "Just students and unicorns, no teachers. We could use the small barn by the stables. It's only got a few bales of hay in it at the moment and no one ever goes there. We're going to have a spooky theme – mix drinks to make a Witch's Brew, make googly eyeballs out of marshmallows and decorate the barn and stables with fake cobwebs. The boys in Topaz dorm said they'd help us organise it. Don't you think it's the

best idea ever?"

"It does sound awesome," Freya agreed. "When?"

"On Wednesday night," said Rosa. "Three days' time."

"But that's Honey's birthday," Freya pointed out.

"Oh." Rosa thought for a second and then her face lit up with a smile. "Well, it can be a birthday party too! Honey would like that, wouldn't she?"

"Yes, I'm sure she would," said Freya. Honey was really lively and loved parties and having fun. "I could give her my present at the party."

Rosa high-fived her. "Perfect! And we can all sing "Happy Birthday" to her at the same time. There's so much to organise!" Her eyes shone – she loved organising things. "We're going to have a planning meeting after dinner tonight in the lounge with Topaz dorm. All of Diamond dorm

have to be there." She saw Freya start to open her mouth to object. "Nope, no excuses allowed," she declared. "You have to be there. Got it?"

Freya sighed. "Got it, Rosa." After having lived with Rosa for ten months she knew there was no point arguing when she was in one of her bossy moods.

Rosa beamed. "Great! This is going to be so much fun!"

After dinner, Diamond dorm met with Topaz dorm to discuss the party. For a brief second, Freya considered slipping away to work on her invention. She was pretty certain she wouldn't be missed. But as she started for the door, Ariana caught her eye. "You're not leaving, are you?"

Busted! Swallowing back a sigh, Freya shook her head. "Course not."

Rosa clapped her hands together. "Listen up

now, everyone. This is a planning meeting for our party. Remember, it's a secret! We don't want the teachers finding out. Right then, let's start with food. What can you all bring?"

"Chocolate!" shouted Himmat.

"Biscuits," said Violet. "My nani just sent me a box."

"Hang on. One at a time," ordered Rosa. "Ariana, please can you write a list of food ideas?"

Ariana waved a notebook in the air. "Already on it."

Once the food had been noted down, Rosa moved on to the other things they needed to do. Ariana turned the page to start a new list.

"Let's pick some purple pumpkins!" said Matilda. "There are some massive ones in the vegetable garden. We could put them in the barn and have a leapfrog race with them."

"Pumpkin picking," said Ariana, furiously writing.

"How about getting some of those giant exploding pea pods?" said Miki. "They're fun. We were playing a game with them the other day seeing who could catch the most peas when each pod exploded."

"Cool. What else?" asked Rosa.

"Get some apples for apple bobbing!"

"And to make toffee apples with!"

As everyone called out ideas, Freya sneaked a look at the clock on the ledge above the fireplace. There was an hour until lights out. She edged towards the door but as she reached for the handle, Rosa called out, "Where are you going, Freya?"

Freya's heart thumped as all eyes turned her way. "I was just going to work on my invention."

"You're always working on it at the moment," said Miki curiously. "What is it?"

Rosa snorted. "There's no way she'll tell. I

15

thought she was going to eat me alive when I tried to go into the workshop this afternoon."

"I'm keeping it secret until Honey's birthday," said Freya, not wanting to admit to everyone that she was hoping it would give her and Honey a chance to bond if it was a perfect surprise.

"Very mysterious," Himmat teased.

Freya rolled her eyes at him and left the room,

but as she shut the door she could still hear them talking. She paused for a moment.

"I wonder why she's being so secretive?" That was Matilda.

"If we knew what it was, then maybe we could help her," said Violet. "She seems quite stressed about it."

"Maybe we should have a little peek at what she's doing?" said Rosa.

Freya's heart started to speed up. No! She didn't want them to! Her friends were the best, but she knew they were all useless at keeping secrets from their unicorns and it would just take one unicorn to accidentally mention something to Honey and then the whole surprise would be spoilt and her chances of bonding with Honey would be ruined. She ran to the workshop, her mind racing. She needed somewhere safer to work, somewhere her robot wouldn't be found until the party.

She threw her tools in her bag and slung it over her shoulder then put a blanket over the robot and heaved it up in her arms. Leaving the workshop, she glanced left and right and, making sure there was no one watching, she made her way up the spiral staircase that led to Diamond dorm. She didn't stop at the dorm though. She kept on going up the tower until she reached a small landing where there was a marble statue of a unicorn's head on a plinth and a large cupboard in the wall. The cupboard was used for storing old packing crates. *I'll put the robot in here for now*, she thought, *and look for somewhere safer to work on it. There must be a quiet room somewhere in the academy I can use.*

The robot was heavy and Freya's arms were aching. With a relieved sigh, she plonked it down, making its wheels clatter loudly on the floor.

"What was that?" She heard Rosa's voice from

the bottom of the staircase.

Freya caught her breath. Oh no! The others must have left the lounge and be on their way up to the dorm. What if they came to see what the noise was? Turning the handle, she opened the cupboard and shoved the robot hastily inside. It trundled forward on its wheels and bumped into a wobbly pile of cardboard boxes. The boxes toppled over.

CRASH!

Freya froze in dismay.

"There's someone up there!" Freya heard Ariana gasp.

"Let's investigate!" cried Matilda. "Come on, everyone!"

Freya frantically leapt into the cupboard and pulled the door shut behind her. Now what was she going to do? She leant against the wall, her heart pounding. Perhaps she could hide behind

the boxes. The robot was still hidden under its blanket. There was a chance they might not find her if she was quiet. Ouch! Something hard stuck into her back. She felt for it with a hand. It was a little lever. Freya pushed it. There was a muffled creak and the wall that Freya was leaning against started to spin slowly like a revolving door. With a startled gasp, Freya fell backwards into thin air!

CHAPTER THREE

Freya stared round. She was in a secret room! The full moon was shining through the cracked glass of a small window, giving her just enough light to see by. The tower room contained only a dusty desk. Shelves lined the curved walls and were packed with glass jars filled with old dried herbs. There were a couple of paintings hung around the room. One was an old picture of a frozen lake but the picture that really caught her attention was a lifelike portrait of a handsome young unicorn with a long golden mane. Stepping closer, Freya saw that the artist had entitled the picture "Prancer". She wondered why it was

hidden away in a secret room.

Before she could think about it any more, she heard the sound of her friends' voices on the other side of the wall in the cupboard. Freya stood like a statue.

"There's no one here." Rosa sounded almost disappointed.

Freya and Honey

"What was that noise then?" said Matilda.

"Maybe some boxes fell over," suggested Violet.

"By themselves?" Rosa didn't sound convinced.

"Well, there's definitely no one up here. Come on, let's go back down to the dorm," said Ariana.

Pressing her ear to the wall, Freya listened as they left the cupboard. She breathed out a

trembling sigh of relief. They hadn't found her or the robot. Phew! As she looked around the room, an idea slowly formed in her mind. This would be a perfect workshop! There was plenty of space to work and she'd be able to get to it really easily from the dorm. Her friends would never find it and she would be able to finish her robot in peace. Then, after Honey's birthday, she could show the room to the rest of Diamond dorm. A grin spread across her face as she imagined how surprised they would be! A secret room – they would love it! She wished she could tell them all straight away, but it was only a few more days to wait.

Going to the revolving wall, she pressed the lever again and spun back into the cupboard. Picking up the robot, she carried it into the secret room. There were some rags on one of the shelves and she used them to wipe away some dust from the desk. As she did so, she saw there were some

strange dark scorch marks on its wooden top as if someone had placed a burning rope on it. Weird. Freya shrugged, maybe someone had been doing secret science experiments up here. She turned to her robot again.

Luckily, the unicorn robot didn't seem to have suffered for being carried around. Freya examined it. It wasn't much to look at. Built from plain grey metal, it had a rectangular face and wonky ears. Its thick neck was bolted to a rectangular body and it held a large basket in its mouth by the handle. Its legs were straight and fixed to a

platform mounted on wheels. The unicorn didn't have a mane or tail, but it was still recognisable, and Freya felt a surge of satisfaction as she examined it. "Not bad! Now I just need to work out why you sometimes run into obstacles in front of you and how to stop you from spinning to the left," she muttered.

It took her a while but eventually Freya worked out how to adjust the sensors she'd fitted so that the unicorn would be able to tell if it needed to stop to avoid crashing into things. It was voice activated. "Robot... Forward!" she commanded.

The unicorn set off on a straight path but then veered off in a circle. Freya stopped it and tipped it up to examine the motor. Humming softly, she selected a screwdriver from her tools. She took her time, carefully laying the screws, cogs and other motor parts beside her on the floor. Everything seemed to be working properly and she was sure it was all in the right place. What else might cause the

unicorn to turn in a circle? The two axles were definitely the same length. She'd measured them twice before she cut them. The wheels were the same diameter, so it couldn't be that either, unless... Freya narrowed her eyes. She'd run out of metal and had to use a new sheet for the last wheel. The metal was a slightly different colour, but it looked the same thickness. She'd been in a rush as usual though, and she hadn't actually measured it. Removing the wheels, she measured them. One wheel was thinner.

"So that's the problem! If I make all the wheels from the new sheet of metal, it should solve it."

As Freya pushed her fringe away from her face, she noticed the black greasy stains on her hands. She'd better wash them before bedtime. "Oh no!" she gasped in alarm. She'd completely lost track of time. Hastily, she packed up her tools. She'd leave everything here and come back as soon as she could.

Freya spun back through the revolving wall. She was just stepping out of the cupboard when Matilda came up the stairs. Her face was pale, and she was holding a washbag high in the air as if it were a dangerous weapon.

"Freya! Phew!" Matilda's breath rushed out with a whoosh. "I heard something moving up here and I thought it was a ghost."

"What would you have done if it *had* been a ghost?" asked Freya.

Matilda grinned. "Run to get the others of course! Anyway, what were you doing?" She frowned. "We heard a noise up there earlier too. Was that you? Why were you in the cupboard?"

"No…" Freya started to deny it but then she gave up. There was no good reason for being in the cupboard, and she knew Matilda would keep asking questions until she cracked! "OK. Busted!" she agreed, lowering her voice to barely a whisper.

"It was me that made the noise when you all came up earlier. Look, Matilda, if you really promise not to tell anyone else, then I'll tell you about something amazing I found."

"I won't," Matilda said instantly. "What is it?"

"It's a secret room with a revolving wall! I'm going to use it as a workshop."

Matilda's eyes grew huge. "Really? That's awesome! Can I see?"

"We'll get into trouble if we're not in bed soon," said Freya, "but I'll show you it tomorrow as long as you promise to keep it a secret."

"OK, I promise!" Matilda breathed.

CHAPTER FOUR

"Today, we are starting a new topic," said Ms Rivers, the strict Geography and Culture teacher. "Open your notebooks and put the heading *Myths and Legends*."

Freya scribbled the words but her mind wasn't really on the lesson. All morning, Matilda had been shooting conspiratorial grins at her. Freya's stomach turned over anxiously. She hoped the others wouldn't notice and ask what was going on. Had she made a big mistake confiding in Matilda? She was great fun but she wasn't the most reliable or secretive person ever. *I wish I hadn't told her,*

thought Freya, as she neatly underlined the title.

"So, who can tell me any myths or legends that we have here on Unicorn Island?" said Ms Rivers.

Isla from Ruby dorm put up her hand. "What about the Frozen Lagoon? That's a myth, isn't it? A bottomless lagoon that's always covered with ice, that's supposed to be on the east coast of Unicorn Island but no one's ever found it."

Valentina, also from Ruby dorm, snorted. "You're as dumb as a flapdoodle, Isla. Everyone knows that's just a made-up story."

"Which is precisely why Isla's suggestion is a very good example of a myth, Valentina," said Ms Rivers sharply. "A myth is a story. It may once have had a grain of truth, but it has been exaggerated and changed over the years. Well done, Isla."

As Ms Rivers turned away, Valentina pulled a face at Isla. "Flapdoodle!" she hissed.

Isla quickly looked down at her desk. Valentina was one of the meanest girls at the school and Freya felt sorry for Isla, Molly and Ana who shared Ruby dorm with her. Valentina was in her second year at the academy because she and her unicorn, Golden Briar, hadn't bonded in the first year. Being a second year seemed to make Valentina bossier and snappier each day.

Miki put up his hand. "I know a myth, Miss," he said.

"Yes, Miki?"

Freya saw Miki's eyes twinkle mischievously. "If you don't graduate from Unicorn Academy at the end of your second year, you turn into a red-bellied slug with four eyes and a pointed nose, so Valentina had better watch out, hadn't she?" He grinned.

Valentina returned his grin with a death glare.

Ms Rivers sighed. "No, Miki, you know you don't. Now, has anyone got anything sensible to contribute?"

Himmat put up his hand. "There's a myth about a ghost that haunts the towers of the academy. It's supposed to be a teacher who once died here. She walks around the corridors and climbs the towers at night."

"Is that true?" said Violet.

Himmat nodded. "My brother thought he saw her when he was here."

"Himmat, that's not quite the kind of myth I was thinking about," said Ms Rivers. "Have any of you heard about the Silver Unicorn? It's a mysterious unicorn who appears occasionally, always first thing in the morning, and anyone

who sees it is blessed with good luck."

Freya made notes as Ms Rivers continued to tell them some of the myths of the land. It was really interesting, and she was surprised when break time came. They all headed to the dining room for cookies and hot chocolate.

"Maybe the noises we heard yesterday from above our dorm were made by the ghost who haunts the school," said Rosa as they left the classroom.

"But ghosts aren't real," Ariana argued.

"Well, something made that noise," Rosa told her.

"There could be another explanation," said Matilda, sending Freya a look.

Freya tensed. Surely Matilda wasn't going to give the game away? "So… Um, when are we going to tell the other dorms about the party?" she said quickly.

To her relief, her change of subject worked. "We'll tell them now – at break," said Rosa. "Most people will be in the hall so we can pass the message round. Come on!"

Matilda grabbed Freya's arm and dropped back as Rosa hurried on with Ariana and Violet. "Can we see the secret room now?" she whispered.

"Now? But we've got cross-country with Ms Tulip after break."

"That's half an hour away. We can have a look and get to the stables in time if we go now."

Freya sighed. "OK. Let's go. But remember you're not to tell anyone."

"I won't," said Matilda.

They peeled away from the others and headed for the spiral staircase.

"In here," said Freya, opening the cupboard.

Matilda raised her eyebrows. "But this is just a cupboard."

"No, it's not. Watch!" Freya went to the wall and pulled the lever. There was a familiar creak. She pressed her back to the wall and felt it start to move.

Matilda squealed as the wall revolved and Freya vanished from sight. Freya hastily pulled the lever again and returned to the cupboard. "So?" she said, her eyes shining.

"Oh. My. Wow!" gasped Matilda, her eyes as wide as saucers. "What's on the other side?"

"Come and see," said Freya, patting the wall beside her.

Matilda ran to stand with Freya and Freya pulled the lever again.

"This is so cool!" Matilda walked around the room, slowly taking it all in. "A secret room." She peered at the bottles and jars on the shelves. "It looks like it used to be a science room or something."

"I know. I'm going to have it as my workshop from now on. I'm working on…" Freya swept the blanket off her invention. "This! It's a birthday present for Honey," she said, as Matilda stared at the robot. She felt suddenly shy. "What do you think?"

"It's incredible," Matilda breathed. "Does it actually move?"

"Yes, it's voice activated and it can fetch things. It puts that basket down, picks things up in its mouth, drops them in the basket and then picks the basket up and carries it back. It needs a bit more work because it keeps turning in circles, but I think I know how to fix that glitch." Freya glanced at Matilda. "I know it doesn't look much like a unicorn but do … do you think Honey will like it?"

"I bet she's going to love it!" Matilda exclaimed. "You're so clever! I don't know how you did it." She walked round it. "It … well … it doesn't look very pretty at the moment though. If you want, I could paint it and give it a mane and tail."

Freya hesitated. She'd never worked on an invention with anyone else before, but Matilda was brilliant at art and she wanted the robot to be as good as possible for Honey. "Yes, please."

"Really?" Matilda looked delighted. "Brilliant! Why don't we sneak away from the others and work on it this evening? I'll bring

my paints and you can bring some biscuits or something."

Freya grinned. "OK, it's a deal!" she said.

CHAPTER FIVE

Cross-country was one of Freya's favourite lessons – she loved galloping and jumping, and Honey loved it too. However, for once she was glad when their lesson finished. If she was going to work on the robot that evening, she needed to get all her homework done during the lunch break.

"Come on, Honey, let's get back to the stables as quickly as we can," she urged.

"Do we have to?" Honey said. "It's a lovely sunny day. We could go to the play park."

"I can't. I need to do my homework," said Freya.

"There's no time for homework now," said Rosa, overhearing. "We agreed to go pumpkin picking with Miki and Himmat this lunchtime, remember? For the party."

Freya groaned inwardly. "Do you really need me? I've got loads to do."

"You have to come and help," said Rosa. "The pumpkins are massive and it's going to take all of us to pick them and take them to the stables."

"OK," sighed Freya.

"As soon as we've settled our unicorns we'll meet at the stable entrance and go to the pumpkin patch," said Rosa, hurrying away.

Honey snorted. "Do you have to go, Freya? We hardly see each other at the moment."

"You see me lots," Freya said.

"Only in lessons. You never visit me the rest of the time. I miss you."

Freya felt guilty. "I promise that I'll change that,

soon," she said. "I'm just really busy working on my invention."

Honey huffed. "I think you like your invention more than you like me."

"I don't!" exclaimed Freya. She wished she could tell Honey that the invention was for her. *It's just a couple more days*, she told herself. *Then Honey will understand.*

"Wow! Look at these pumpkins!" said Freya a little while later, as she stared at the sea of massive purple pumpkins in the walled vegetable garden. She picked her way carefully between the pumpkins, trying not to let their curly green tendrils trip her up.

Miki stopped beside a huge pumpkin. "Someone help me here."

Himmat rushed over and held the pumpkin while Miki cut through its thick spikey stem. Then

42

Freya and Honey

Freya and Rosa helped them to lift it into Miki's wheelbarrow. Pumpkin picking took much longer than Freya had expected but they had a good haul of pumpkins to show for it. They carted them to the stables in the wheelbarrows.

"Goodness me! What are you going to do with all those?" Ms Willow, the school nurse, came out of her unicorn's stable with some rolls of ribbon in her hands. She was young and pretty and the girls really liked her. She was always fussing over her unicorn, Daffodil, decorating her yellow and

orange mane with elaborate plaits or pottering around the gardens with her, gathering herbs to make medicines from. Daffodil had healing magic but Ms Willow liked to use herbal medicines on sick or injured students whenever possible so as not to tire Daffodil out. She really did adore her little unicorn!

"We're going to use them to play a game of leapfrog in the small barn, Miss," said Rosa. The others exchanged grins. Rosa had conveniently missed out the vital fact that it was going to be a *midnight* game!

"In the barn?" Ms Willow said in surprise. "Why not outside?"

"Just in case it rains," Rosa invented. "It's all right if we play in the barn, isn't it? It's never used for anything."

Ms Willow smiled. "It's fine. Enjoy yourselves!" She headed into the tack room.

Freya and Honey

Diamond and Topaz dorm wheeled the pumpkins into the old stone barn and arranged them around the empty space. Their unicorns came out of their stalls to watch.

"They're massive!" said Crystal, Rosa's unicorn.

Rosa nodded. "They're going to be perfect for playing leapfrog." She tried to leapfrog a huge one and got stuck on top of it. She collapsed to the ground, giggling.

Freya suddenly realised Honey hadn't come outside with everyone else. She went to find her. Honey was in her stall, picking at a net of hay. She looked unhappy.

"Are you OK?" Freya said. "Don't you want to

come and see the pumpkins we collected?"

Honey looked at her reproachfully. "Freya, we'll never bond if you keep secrets from me."

Freya suddenly stood very still. "Secrets? What do you mean?"

"I overheard Matilda telling Pearl that she's working on a top-secret project with you and only the two of you know what it is. If you were going to tell anyone about it, Freya, it should have been me."

Freya's cheeks turned hot. She should *never* have trusted Matilda! "Matilda wasn't supposed to say anything to anyone," she said angrily. "She promised! Did she say what the project was?"

Honey shook her head. "No, she wouldn't let on. Pearl tickled her with her tail and Matilda laughed so hard she got hiccups, but she still wouldn't say."

Freya's anger faded slightly. At least Matilda

hadn't let on what the secret was.

"Will you tell me the secret too?" Honey asked.

Freya hated seeing Honey upset but she desperately wanted the present to be an amazing surprise. *Just two more days and then she'll realise why I kept it secret,* she thought. "I'm sorry," she said. "I can't." She reached out to stroke Honey, but Honey stepped away.

"Don't be like that, Honey," Freya pleaded.

Suddenly, a flash of violet lit up the stable. A second later there was a huge bang from the direction of the barn. It was followed by a series of smaller bangs and shrieks. A thin wisp of smoke curled into the stable. Freya's nose wrinkled. Burnt pumpkin with a whiff of sugar! She rushed from Honey's box and into the barn. Miki and Himmat were standing in the middle of it looking like they'd fallen into a gloopy purple swamp. They were covered in pumpkin flesh and flat pale seeds and the girls were crowding round them.

"Gross!" A lump of goo slid from Himmat's hands and on to his boots.

"*Aaaatishoo! Atishoo!*" Miki sneezed violently. "That's better," he finally gasped. "I had a

pumpkin seed stuck up my nose!"

Ms Willow came running in. "What just happened? Miki, Himmat, are you both OK?"

"The pumpkins exploded!" Miki exclaimed. "Himmat and I were moving them and suddenly they went bang!"

"Boom!" said Himmat. "Pow! Pumpkin everywhere!"

Ms Willow looked dismayed. "You poor things. The pumpkins must have been rotten and in the warmth of the barn they exploded. Pumpkins are really best kept outside. It was lucky no one was hurt. Go and have a wash, boys. Everyone else, please help clear up."

Freya grabbed a shovel and began to scrape up the splattered pumpkins. "I don't understand," she said to Ariana, who was clearing up nearby. "The pumpkins were fresh from the field and the insides don't smell rotten."

Ariana frowned. "So, what are you saying?"

"I'm not sure. It's just, when the pumpkins exploded, I smelt something sweet. It reminded me of magic."

Rosa overheard. "Maybe it was Twinkle or Honey discovering their magic powers."

"What? The power of exploding vegetables?" said Violet, her eyebrows shooting up. "I've not heard of that before."

Rosa giggled. "OK, maybe not."

"So, what did make them explode?" said Ariana.

Matilda's eyes widened. "It could have been a spell or an enchantment."

"But who would enchant a load of pumpkins to

explode?" said Freya.

"Someone could be trying to wreck the party," said Ariana. "How about Valentina?" she gasped.

"But her unicorn, Golden Briar, has wind power, nothing to do with exploding things," said Violet. "And Valentina can't cast spells – only people who have a spell-weaver unicorn can do that."

"Also, *why* would Valentina do something like that?" said Rosa. "We invited her to the party at break time and, even though she was a bit snooty about it, she said she'd come. Why would she try to wreck the party?"

"Oh, I don't know," said Ariana. "You're right, it doesn't make sense. Maybe the pumpkins were rotten after all." She sighed and looked around. "I guess we'd better clear up."

CHAPTER SIX

"I think I've done it." Freya tightened the last screw then sat back on her heels.

"Let's try it out." Matilda, who had a smudge of paint on her nose, stopped painting.

Freya faced the robot. "Robot… On," she said, clearly. With a small hum the robot came to life. "Robot… Forward," she added.

The robot jerked then trundled forward, rolling across the smooth wooden floor. It went in a perfectly straight line towards the enormous blocked-up fireplace, no spinning or turning. Freya held her breath as it got closer to the fireplace. Was it going

to crash? No! It swung round just in time and continued around the room.

"It's working!" Freya said in excitement. "Robot… Stop!" she commanded. The robot came to a standstill. "I did it!" Freya clapped a hand to her mouth.

"Hurrah!" Matilda waved her paintbrush in the air. "You're a genius!" She threw her arms round Freya and hugged her.

Freya stiffened for a second, but Matilda didn't seem to notice and, after a second, Freya found herself hugging her rather gingerly back.

"Is that all the engineering work done?" asked Matilda. "Can I paint the rest of it now?"

"Yes," Freya stood back and squinted at the robot. "Do you think Honey will like it?"

"She's going to love, love, LOVE it!" exclaimed Matilda. "All the unicorns are going to want one and…"

TAP. TAP. TAP.

A noise came from the fireplace. Matilda and Freya froze.

"What was that?" whispered Matilda.

"I don't know," Freya whispered back.

"Could it be a bird? We had one stuck in our chimney once," Matilda said.

Freya went over to the fireplace and peered at the wooden board blocking it. She realised

something.
"This isn't
just a piece
of wood –
there are
hinges on
one side
and a button on the other. It's a door!" She put
her hand on it.

Whooooooooooo! A long drawn-out moan
echoed out from behind it.

Freya sprang back.

"It's a ghost!" squeaked Matilda. "I bet it's the
ghost of the dead teacher that Himmat told us
about! Quick, Freya, let's get out of here!" She raced
to the revolving wall. Freya darted beside her and
pressed the lever. The wall turned and they found
themselves in the dark of the cupboard. Both of
them were breathing hard and their faces were pale.

"We heard a g ... ghost!" stammered Matilda. "A real ghost!"

But now she was out of the room, Freya's panic was dying down and her logical brain was kicking in. "It can't have been," she said, feeling a bit silly for running away like that. "Ghosts don't exist. It must have been a bird."

"A bird that says *whoooooooo?*" said Matilda. She shook her head. "No. I think it was a ghost and we should tell the others."

"No!" Freya said sharply. "They'll only want to come to the room and then they'll see the robot. Please, Matilda, don't say anything until after the party – that will also give us a chance to check if we hear anything again. If we tell them it's a ghost and it is just a bird, then we'll look really stupid."

"OK," Matilda agreed reluctantly.

They hurried downstairs to the dorm. Rosa,

Violet and Ariana were sitting on the floor making enormous paper spiders to decorate the barn for the party. With its cosy rug, pink, lilac and silver duvet covers and sparkling fairy lights the dorm looked wonderfully cosy and safe. Freya felt a rush of relief until the other three looked up with cross expressions.

"Where have you two been?" Rosa demanded. "You were supposed to be helping us make decorations tonight."

"Whoops, sorry!" Matilda looked contrite. "I completely forgot. I'll help now!" She sat down and quickly picked up some scissors.

"It's not fair for you both to let us do all the work for the party," said Rosa, fixing Freya with a look. "There's loads to do."

"I know," said Freya. "And I do want to help. It's just, I've got to finish my invention."

"Because that's more important than anything,

isn't it?" said Rosa. "Freya, have you seen how sad Honey's looking? I guess you can't have done, or you'd have been in the stables, spending time with her this evening rather than with your invention."

A guilty blush warmed Freya's cheeks. "Honey understands," she said defensively, squashing down thoughts of Honey's upset face that afternoon. "She knows this is really important to me. As soon as it's done, I'll be able to spend more time with her, so stop having a go at me."

"Rosa didn't mean to upset you…" Violet started to say.

"I did!" Rosa interrupted. "Honey's sad and we're doing all the work for the party – Freya's being selfish!"

Anger boiled in Freya's stomach. "That's not fair! I—"

A loud crash from the landing above interrupted her.

"What was that?" gasped Ariana.

Matilda's eyes flew to Freya's and Freya knew they were both thinking about the noises they'd heard in the secret room.

Rosa raced to the door, the argument temporarily forgotten. "Let's find out!"

They scrambled for the stairs Rosa reached the landing first. "The statue!" she exclaimed, pointing at the marble unicorn lying on the floor outside the cupboard door.

For a moment they all fell silent. "OK," said Violet slowly. "How can it have fallen over all by itself?"

"The same way the boxes in the cupboard just

toppled over all by themselves," said Ariana, her eyes widening.

"It's a ghost!" squeaked Matilda.

Freya's thoughts raced. The cardboard boxes had been her fault, but what about this? "It can't be a ghost," she said quickly. "Ghosts aren't real." But, even to her ears, her words didn't sound that convincing.

Rosa went to pick it up. "Gosh, it's heavy!"

"Let me help." Freya heaved the statue up with Rosa. As they set it on its pedestal, their eyes met for a second. Freya felt her earlier anger fade away. Of course Rosa had been cross with her. It was only because she was worried about Honey and because she wanted the party to be a success. She sighed. "I'm sorry I haven't been helping more, Rosa. I thought you were all having fun planning the party and it didn't matter if I wasn't involved."

"We have been having fun," said Rosa. "But it would be even more fun if you were properly involved too."

Freya nodded. "I will be from now on. I promise."

"And what about Honey?" said Rosa.

"I'll spend more time with her and get her present finished too. When she sees it, if she likes it enough, then maybe … well, maybe we'll finally bond." Freya struggled to say the last words out loud. She hated admitting her feelings to people, even her friends.

Rosa's expression softened. "So that's why you're working so hard on it? Because you think it might help you bond with her?"

Freya nodded.

Rosa sighed. "If I'd known that, I wouldn't have given you such a hard time for not helping out. Sorry, Freya."

"I'm sorry too," Freya said. "And from now on, I promise I'll help out more." They exchanged smiles.

"I've just thought of something," said Ariana as they headed back to the dorm.

"What?" said Violet.

"Well, if ghosts aren't real then whoever pushed over the statue and those boxes has to be a person, doesn't it?"

"Like a student or a teacher, you mean?" said Violet.

Ariana bit her lip. "Or the cloaked figure."

They stared at her. "The cloaked figure who was draining magic from the Heart Tree and the waterfall?" echoed Matilda. "You think she could be here in the school?"

Ariana nodded. "She could be the one who made the pumpkins explode too."

"But why?" said Freya logically. "It doesn't make

sense. Draining magic from the environment – that's proper big, bad evil. Why would the cloaked figure come here to knock over statues and make pumpkins explode? It's not the same kind of thing."

"I suppose," said Ariana, relaxing slightly.

"Freya's right. I bet it's not her. But if she *does* come to the school, she'd better watch out because we'll catch her!" declared Rosa. "Won't we, Diamond dorm?" She held her hand up.

"Definitely!" everyone chorused, meeting her hand with a group high-five.

CHAPTER SEVEN

"Even *more* pumpkins?" Ms Willow said, looking into the barn with Daffodil, as Diamond dorm unloaded a whole load of new pumpkins at lunchtime the next day.

"We thought we'd try again," said Rosa brightly. "We really do want to play leapfrog."

Ms Willow's eyes strayed to one of the big hay bales where they had put a pile of decorations and torches. "Hmm. Something is telling me that you might have something more planned than just a simple game of leapfrog, girls." A smile tugged at her mouth. "It's OK" she said. "I won't tell

anyone. Your secret's safe with me."

She left the barn with Daffodil. Exchanging relieved looks, Freya and the others began to unload the pumpkins.

Later that afternoon, Freya and Matilda headed up to the secret room. Freya's skin prickled as the wall revolved. Would they hear any strange spooky noises again? But all was quiet, and she gradually started to relax.

"There!" said Matilda eventually, standing back and admiring the robot. She had given it a felt mane and tail and painted its body with delicate swirls of colour.

"It looks awesome now. Thanks, Matilda," said Freya gratefully.

"It's been fun," said Matilda. "You're so clever, Freya. I don't know anyone else who could build a robot."

Freya's heart swelled with pride. Building the robot had been her biggest project so far. She couldn't quite believe she'd actually done it. And she couldn't wait for Honey to see it the following night. *Oh, please let her love it*, she thought.

She began picking up her tools from the floor. As she did so, her eyes fell on the fireplace. With everything that had happened she had completely

forgotten that she had found out that the board blocking the fireplace was actually a door. She went over to examine it. Yes, there were definitely hinges and an indent that looked like a button on the other side.

"What are you doing?" Matilda asked, as Freya explored the indent with her fingers.

"Just investigating." Freya pressed. There was a click and the door in the fireplace swung open.

Matilda gasped as a blast of cold musty air wafted into the room. "It's a door!"

Freya peered inside. "And look what's behind it. A tunnel!" A dark tunnel with stone walls and a low ceiling sloped steeply downwards.

Matilda joined her. "Where do you think it goes to?"

Freya glanced at her. "We could find out."

"But what if we meet a ghost?" said Matilda.

"We won't. Ghosts don't exist," Freya said

67

firmly. Now she could see a tunnel she felt much happier. A tunnel behind the fireplace explained things. Someone – a person – could have come up it and tapped on the door and made noises to scare them. OK, she had no idea *why* someone would do that but at least it was a theory that she could believe.

She fetched a torch from her tool bag. "Are you coming with me?"

Matilda followed Freya through the fireplace and into the stone tunnel. Even with the light of the torch it was hard to see what was ahead of them. They were definitely heading downwards, fast. Where were they going to end up?

Freya heard the drip of water. It grew louder as they continued walking and the floor levelled out. Suddenly the tunnel opened up into a small chamber. Freya shone the torch around. There were two more passageways leading away from

the chamber and multicoloured water was dripping down the walls, forming puddles on the floor.

"I reckon the tunnel has brought us out of the school and through the gardens," she said. "I think we're under Sparkle Lake."

"I wonder where those tunnels go to?" said Matilda, pointing at the other two passageways.

"Only one way to find out," said Freya with a

grin. This was exciting! She headed down the left-hand tunnel, which was slightly wider and higher. For a while it went straight and then it started to slope upwards.

"Oh, no. It's a dead end," said Matilda, as they reached a stone wall.

Freya shone the torch on the wall. The beam revealed some hand- and footholds carved into the stone. Glancing up, she caught her breath. Above them there was a trapdoor with light shining around the edges of it. "Look!" She stood on tiptoe and ran her hands over the wooden surface. Finding a small indent, she pressed it. There was a faint click and she felt the trapdoor loosen. She heaved upwards and it opened.

Freya pulled herself up the wall using the hand- and footholds and climbed out. "We're in the barn!"

The trapdoor was hidden away in a dark corner

of the barn. A layer of straw had been covering it. *I guess that's why we never noticed it,* thought Freya.

"Wow!" Matilda breathed, climbing out. "A secret passageway from our tower all the way to the stables! Isn't this brilliant? Just wait until we tell the others!"

"After the party," said Freya quickly. "Or they'll want to explore it and see the secret room. It's perfect! I was wondering how to get my robot out to the barn without anyone seeing. Well, I can use this passageway!"

"Should we go and see Pearl and Honey while we're here?" said Matilda.

Freya hesitated. Honey had been really distant and reserved with her ever since the day before. "Um, let's not," she said quickly, not wanting another awkward encounter. "We should go back and get ready for supper before anyone starts

looking for us."

"OK." Matilda grinned at Freya. "A secret room *and* secret tunnels! How amazing is that?"

CHAPTER EIGHT

After supper, there was a knock on Diamond dorm's door. It was Isla and Molly from Ruby dorm. "We've made some cakes," said Isla shyly. She opened the lid of a massive cake tin full of spider cupcakes.

"And toffee apples," added Molly, holding out a plate. "We thought we'd take them to the stables now. Is that OK?"

"Sure, we'll come with you if you like? We can finish off putting up the decorations," said Rosa.

They all headed down to the barn. On the way, they stopped at the stables to say hello to their

unicorns. All the unicorns trotted out of their stalls to greet their riders – all apart from Honey.

Freya went into her stall. Honey's nostrils fluttered in a whicker but then she seemed to stop herself, turning it into an unhappy snort.

"Honey, don't be like this," begged Freya. "Please." She went over and stroked her, but Honey turned away.

Freya's heart twisted in her chest. She knew Honey's feelings had been badly hurt. She wanted to say she was sorry and tell her how much she loved her, but it was so hard to put her feelings into words. She wished she could be more like Matilda and just blurt out whatever she was thinking.

Instead, she cleared her throat and picked up Honey's water bucket. "I'll get you some more water," she said.

She scrubbed the bucket and refilled it, then put more sky berries in Honey's manger and fluffed up the straw in her bed. "I'll ... um, see you tomorrow then," she said, hesitating in the doorway, desperately wanting to say more.

Honey gave a small nod. Walking away unhappily, Freya joined the others, who were now decorating. By the time they had finished, the barn looked amazing, covered with fake cobwebs, giant spiders, cut-out ghosts and cauldrons. There were hay bales to sit on, pumpkins set out for leapfrog racing, a load of popping pea pods and a massive pile of apples on one of the straw bales ready to be put in a bucket for apple bobbing.

Rosa looked around and gave a happy sigh.

"You know, I really think this is going to be the best party ever!"

Freya didn't sleep very well that night. She kept thinking about Honey and how miserable she had looked. She had pictured over and over again the grand moment when she would pull the blanket off the robot, revealing it to Honey in front of everyone. She had imagined Honey's delighted face and a strand of her own blonde hair turning red and gold like Honey's mane as they bonded. She really wanted that, but she didn't think she could bear another day of Honey looking so miserable. *Maybe I should just forget about the surprise and tell her what I've been doing*, she thought. She tossed and turned and by daybreak had made a decision. She was going to tell Honey what she'd been doing even if it meant ruining their chance to bond. She couldn't carry on making her unhappy.

Leaving the others asleep in the dorm, she

crept out to the hallway. But as she headed down the staircase, she heard footsteps at the bottom. She froze. It must be a teacher! Moving as silently as she could, she went back up the stairs, past the dorm and into the secret room.

Letting herself into it, her eyes fell on the robot. An idea formed in her mind. Why didn't she take the robot to Honey now? After all, it was Honey's birthday already. There was no reason she had to wait until the party that evening. *I'll do it*, she thought, feeling a rush of excitement. Tucking the blanket under her arm and getting her torch and some rope from the toolbox, she lifted the robot into the tunnel.

"Robot... Forward!" she commanded. The robot started to trundle down the slope at her side, its wheels clattering on the stone.

When they reached the chamber under the lake, Freya glanced at the right-hand passageway. Where did it lead to? If the stables were to the left, then

the right must lead in the direction of the walled vegetable garden. Curiosity pricked at her, but she shook her head. No, there was no time to explore it. She needed to get to Honey and explain.

A noise came from the tunnel behind her. Freya swung round just as a stone bounced out of it into the chamber. She stiffened.

"Is anyone there?" she demanded, stepping forwards bravely.

There was no answer. Freya breathed out in relief. The stone must just have been dislodged by the robot's wheels. "Robot… Forward!" she said, turning it towards the passageway that led to the barn. The robot trundled on.

It was tricky getting it through the trapdoor at the end but with the rope she managed to heave it into the barn. As she climbed out, an idea formed in her head. Maybe she could reveal the robot to Honey in here and still make it a bit of a surprise?

She put the robot in the centre of the barn, covered it with the blanket and headed towards the door, but as she did so there was a flash of violet light from the direction of the tunnel. She swung round.

POP! POP! POP!

The pea pods that were piled on one of the hay bales started to explode, the peas whizzing through the air like marbles fired from a catapult. "Ow!" gasped Freya as one giant pea hit her and then another and another. She dodged from side to side as the peas bounced into the opposite wall. What was happening? To her horror, she saw one of the pumpkins start to swell. The pile of apples next to the pea pods started to shake and then an apple suddenly exploded off the pile and shot straight towards her head!

CHAPTER NINE

Freya squealed and ducked just in time but then another apple smashed into her arm, making her yell in pain. She needed to get out of here!

Suddenly there was the sound of clattering hooves and Honey came bursting into the barn. She swerved around the giant pumpkin that was starting to expand and galloped up to Freya. "Freya! I thought I heard you! What's the matter? What's – ow!" she whinnied as an apple hit her neck.

She swung round just as the whole pile of apples exploded into the air. Honey leapt in front

of Freya, batting away the flying apples with her hooves. She moved so quickly, she was like a blur. Sparks flew up around her and the smell of burnt sugar filled the air as she swiped apple after apple away. Finally, the last apple hit the wall and Honey stopped. "What's going on, Freya?" she panted.

"I don't know. I —" Freya's eyes widened in horror as she realised the giant purple pumpkin behind Honey was almost at bursting point. "Honey! Watch out! Get behind me!"

Honey leapt towards Freya and swung round.

Freya's mind raced. If the pumpkin exploded in the barn, it would ruin everything — all the decorations and food would be spoilt and chunks of the pumpkin would hit her and Honey. There was only one thing for it. She pulled the blanket off the robot.

"What's that?" gasped Honey.

Freya didn't have time to reply. "Robot... On!"

she cried. "Robot... Forward!" The robot started to trundle forwards, heading straight for the expanding pumpkin! "Robot... Faster! Robot... DON'T STOP!" Freya shouted.

The robot increased its speed, getting faster and faster. Freya tensed. Would the voice command override the sensors? "Robot... Keep going!" she yelled.

SMASH! The robot barrelled into the pumpkin at top speed, sending it flying backwards. As the pumpkin sailed out of the door, it exploded. Purple goo shot into the air and covered the robot. The robot made a chugging, whining noise and ground to a halt.

For a moment there was total silence.

"OK," said Honey, breaking the silence. "What's going on?"

"Oh, Honey!" Freya flung her arms around Honey's neck. She held Honey tightly, burying

her face in her soft silky mane. "I'm so glad you're not hurt."

Honey nuzzled her. "And I'm glad you're all right too. I heard you scream."

Freya pulled back and looked at her. "You were brilliant. The way you swiped all those apples was incredible. How did you move so fast?"

"I think it might be my magic," said Honey.

"Your magic?" gasped Freya.

"Yes, I felt like I could just suddenly move so much faster than normal."

Freya blinked. "I did see sparks and smelt sugar. That must have been you! Speed magic! Oh, wow!"

"We can try it out again later and see if I'm right, but first you have to tell me what's going on," said Honey. "Why were you here so early and what's *that*?" she said, nodding at the sticky purple robot.

Freya quickly explained about the passageway. "I couldn't sleep so I used it to come here secretly so I could explain why I've not been spending time with you. The secret invention I've been working on is a present for you." She sighed and walked over to the robot. "Or at least it was. It was a unicorn robot that could bring you treats and things."

"A unicorn robot? For me?" Honey stared at her as if she couldn't believe it.

Freya nodded. "I was planning to give it to you at the party. I really wanted it to be the best surprise ever because…" She bit her lip. "Well, I thought if I made you really happy, we might bond." Tears pricked her eyes. She quickly blinked them back. She hated crying but now everything was ruined and she couldn't stop herself.

"Freya." There was a strange note in Honey's voice. Freya looked up at her. "We *have* bonded!"

said Honey. Her eyes sparkled. "Look at your hair!"

Freya glanced down at her hair. On one side there was a bright streak of red and gold. She gasped.

Honey nuzzled her. "I always knew we would."

"What's going on?"

Hearing Rosa's voice, Freya looked round. Diamond dorm were approaching the barn on their unicorns. They cantered up.

Matilda shrieked.

"Your hair, Freya! You've bonded!"

"Yes, and Honey's found her magic!" Freya quickly explained everything, about the invention and her work with Matilda and what had just happened in the barn, with Honey chipping in. The others' eyes grew wider and wider.

"Speed magic – that's awesome!" said Violet.

"You knew Freya was building a robot, you helped her and didn't tell us?" Ariana said, looking at Matilda in astonishment.

"It was soooo hard not to. I wanted to but I promised Freya I wouldn't," said Matilda. "So, who do you think made the vegetables explode?" she asked Freya.

Freya had already come to a conclusion. "I think it's someone who doesn't want people in this barn."

"But why? No one ever uses it," said Violet.

Freya knew it was time to tell the others the

truth. "That's not quite true. There's a trapdoor at the back of the barn. It leads to a secret passageway that comes out in a chamber under the lake. Another passageway from it leads to a secret room hidden behind the cupboard above our dorm and there's a third passageway I haven't explored. I think someone wanted us out of the barn so they could use the trapdoor. I think they've also been trying to scare Matilda and me away from the secret room by pretending to be a ghost."

The others gaped.

"This is really serious. We need to tell the teachers that someone's been sneaking around the school," said Ariana.

"Agreed. But before we do that, I absolutely have to see these secret tunnels!" said Rosa.

Freya led the way to the trapdoor. Rosa peered down it.

"You said there's another tunnel you haven't

been down yet. Let's explore it and see where it goes!"

"What about us?" said Honey anxiously, looking round at the other unicorns. "We can't get down there with you."

"I think the third tunnel might come out somewhere near the vegetable garden," said Freya. "Why don't you all head in that direction and keep listening for us? We'll call you when we find our way out to the surface."

The unicorns nodded.

The girls dropped down through the trapdoor. "Quiet, now!" hissed Freya.

"The person who cast a spell on the vegetables might be somewhere down here. I'm sure I heard them following me before."

They cautiously made their way along the tunnel. When they reached the chamber under the lake, they paused. "That's the tunnel I haven't been down," said Freya in a low voice.

Rosa pointed to the ground. "Hey, look! Footprints!"

The others joined her. Someone had walked through one of the puddles on the floor near the tunnel the girls had just come out of and left a trail of footprints leading into the unexplored tunnel.

Matilda crouched down. "It's a really unusual footprint. The soles of the person's shoes have diamond shapes on." She pulled a pencil out from behind her ear and the notebook she always carried out from her pocket and quickly sketched it.

"It must be the person who did the magic and attacked Freya," said Violet.

"Let's follow the trail!" said Rosa.

"OK, but we need to be even quieter!" hissed Ariana. "The person could be lying in wait for us."

They headed cautiously along the tunnel. It went straight for a while and then slanted upwards.

"Look! There's a light!" whispered Violet.

"I think it's the end of the tunnel," said Freya.

She was right. The tunnel ended in a wall with a gap at one side. They squeezed through it and found themselves standing on damp soil, hidden behind a huge bush. Freya pushed her way around it and stepped out. Where were they?

She saw a brick wall to one side of them, and realised it was the wall of the vegetable garden. They were standing outside the far end of it. Looking to her left she could see the stables in the distance and

the unicorns trotting in their direction.

"Honey!" Freya shouted, waving. "Honey! We're over here!" Honey lifted her head and started cantering. The others followed her.

"Freya! Look!" cried Rosa. She was pointing in the other direction. Her voice rose. "It's the cloaked figure!"

Freya gasped. A cloaked figure on a tall unicorn with a golden mane and tail was trotting away across the grounds.

"Honey!" she yelled, turning to look at the group of unicorns cantering towards them from the stables. "HURRY!"

CHAPTER TEN

Honey's ears pricked and gold and purple sparks shot up from her hooves. She leapt forward and suddenly she was just a blur leaving the other unicorns far behind. Freya gasped as just a few seconds later Honey arrived beside her. "What is it?" she asked Freya.

Freya was already vaulting on to her back. "We have to catch that cloaked figure!" she said, grabbing Honey's mane. "Gallop as fast as you can!"

Whoosh! The noise came from Honey's hooves. More sparks exploded into the air and the next second Freya felt cold air rushing

past her face so fast it made her eyes stream. She could feel Honey's muscles bunching and stretching, hear the pounding of her hooves. She realised they had left the others far behind and were gaining on the unknown unicorn.

"Keep going, Honey!" Freya yelled.

They thundered on, drawing closer to the figure with every stride. "Stop!" she yelled. "You can't escape from us!" The figure turned and made a flicking motion with one hand. Sparks flew up and a sheet of thick ice instantly covered the ground behind her unicorn's hooves.

"Honey! Whoa!" Freya shrieked. If Honey galloped on to the ice, she would slip and fall and quite possibly break a leg. Honey skidded to a halt, stopping millimetres away from where the ice began. Freya almost catapulted over Honey's head but managed to hang on to her mane and pull herself down on to Honey's back. She looked up.

"They've gone!" she gasped. There was nothing there. The figure, her unicorn – and the ice – had all vanished into thin air!

Honey gasped for breath and staggered.

Freya jumped off her. "Honey, are you all right?"

"Just tired," Honey said, drawing in deep breaths. "It was doing all the magic. I'll be OK soon."

Freya hugged her. "You were amazing. Your magic is the best! We went so fast."

Honey whickered. "It was fun, wasn't it?"

Just then, the rest of Diamond dorm came galloping up.

"Where's the figure gone?" demanded Rosa.

Freya quickly explained what had happened. "I guess the ice must have just been a glamour – an illusion. We could have kept on going."

"You weren't to know," said Violet. "And you were right not to risk it."

"I wonder how the figure just vanished," said Freya. "One second she and her unicorn were there and the next they weren't."

Rosa looked around. "I can't see anywhere there might be another tunnel or passageway. She may have used magic to disappear. She's done it before remember, when we saw her in the woods."

The others nodded. "We have to go and tell Ms Nettles about this," said Ariana.

"Then we'll need to clear up the barn," said Rosa.

"I really want to fix the robot before tonight," added Freya.

"I'll help you clean it up," offered Matilda.

They went back to the stables. Freya gave

Honey an extra ration of sky berries to help her recover her strength. Then she went to find Ms Nettles with the others. Ms Nettles listened seriously, peering down her glasses at the girls as they related their adventure.

"Thank you, Diamond dorm," she said when they'd finished explaining. "You certainly have a knack for getting into adventures. I'll look into all this. This cloaked figure appears to have a very detailed knowledge of the school, which is extremely worrying. We must put some protection spells on these tunnels so that no one can use them to get into the school again. But now," she raised her eyebrows, "can you please explain to me why you had pumpkins, peas and apples in the barn?"

Rosa sighed. "We were planning a party. A spooky midnight feast." Ms Nettles' eyebrows almost hit her hairline. "We're sorry," Rosa rushed on. "It's just that everyone's been so tense since

the camping trip we thought it would be good to have something fun to do."

"It was my idea," said Matilda.

"But we were all involved," said Freya, not wanting Matilda and Rosa to get into trouble on their own.

"Hmmm." Ms Nettles adjusted her glasses. "Well, maybe this once – just this once – I shall overlook the breach of school rules. You may still have your party – but not at midnight! I want you all in bed by ten o'clock at the latest. Agreed?"

They all exchanged delighted looks. "Agreed!" they chorused.

The party was a huge success. All the dorms came. There was lots of laughter and teasing, especially when Matilda almost fell in the barrel of water while bobbing for apples. They played "squeak little ghost" and "find the spider", shouting out clues until everyone was hoarse. Honey showed off her new speed magic by whizzing around, catching peas in her mouth as people fired them from exploding pods. Then they sang "Happy Birthday" to her, and Freya, who'd managed to clean up the robot, trundled it round the barn with a basket full of toffee apples. Everyone was very impressed as they took one to eat.

"Everyone wants a robot now!" Honey said to Freya in delight.

When the games were finally over, Freya sat on top of a massive hay bale with the rest of her dorm, tucking into plates of delicious food. The unicorns stood around them, tearing off big mouthfuls of the hay.

"So, who do we think the mysterious cloaked figure is?" Rosa asked, waving a spider cupcake. "What have they got against our school?"

"Could it be Ms Primrose's friend?" Violet asked, licking a toffee apple. "When she was the

head teacher here, someone was helping her to do bad things, and they were never caught."

"It might be," said Rosa. "We need to keep a careful watch for anything suspicious."

"Yes, we're not going to let anyone do anything to the academy. Diamond dorm will stop them!" Freya declared.

The rest of Diamond dorm cheered, and the unicorns whinnied.

Honey reached her nose up to Freya. "I love my unicorn robot. Thanks, Freya, this is my best birthday ever."

"For the best unicorn ever." Freya jumped down from the bale and kissed her forehead. "I'm sorry I made you sad. I promise nothing will ever come between us again."

Honey softly nuzzled Freya's hair. "Not even a robot?"

"Not even a robot!" Freya grinned.

PRINCESS of PETS

Look out for a BRILLIANT new Nosy Crow series from the author of The Rescue Princesses!

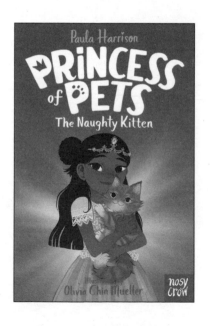
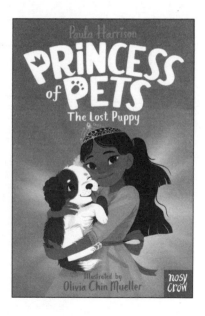

Animal adventures, friendship and a royal family!

LOOK OUT FOR

MAX
The
DETECTIVE CAT

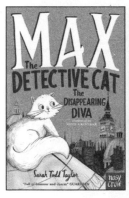 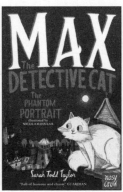 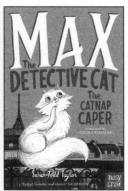

He's the clever cat who puts
the miaow into mystery!

Another MAGICAL
series from Nosy Crow!

SNOW SiSTERS